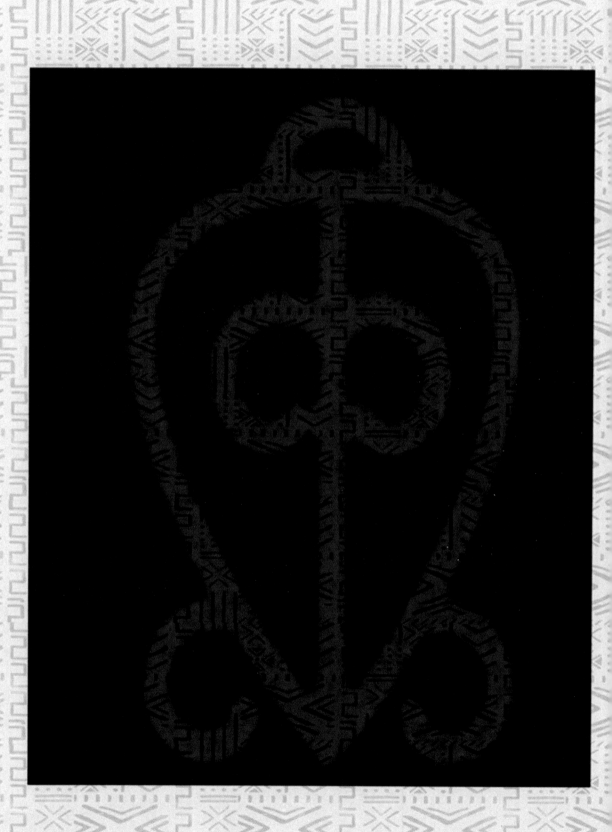

DEAR BLACK BOY

This book is dedicated to
every little Black boy
who has ever felt
unloved,
unseen,
and unheard.
We love you.
We see you.
We hear you.

ISBN: 978- 0-578-91778-8

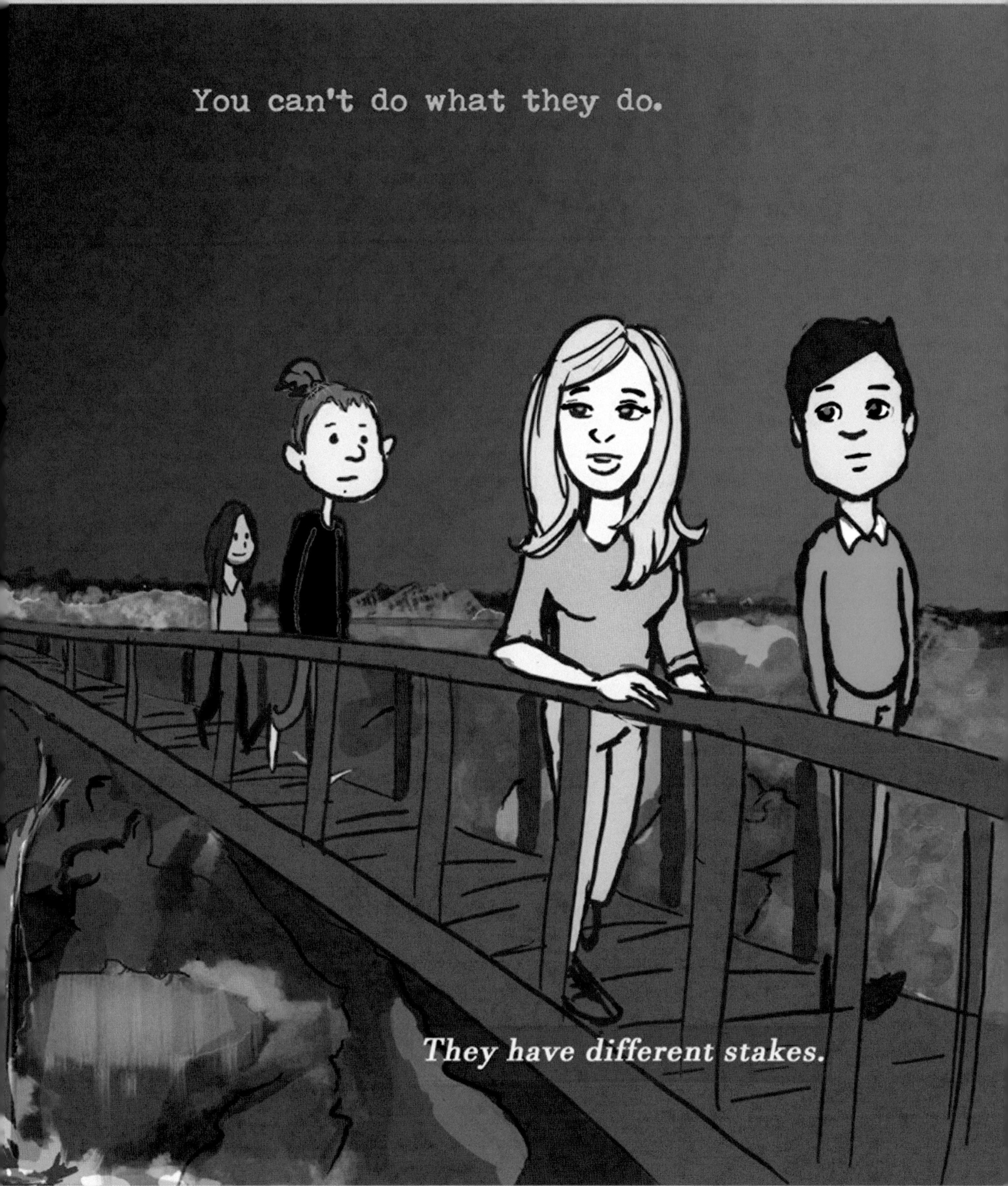
You can't do what they do.
They have different stakes.

Little Black boy,
go to the store.

Keep your head up,
no hoods,
no eyes to the floor.

Little Black boy,
take the car for a drive.

Drive slow,
full stops
and
come home alive.

recite the steps at a stop.

Little Black boy,
who dominates the track,

Never jog in a neighborhood where you might be too black.

If the death of
Black boys
were fire,
America would be hot.

BLACK
LIV
MA

Little Black boy, I know it's not fair.

But the world doesn't love you the way that we care.

Little Black boy,

you are loved ...

you are wanted ...

... the best thing I've ever done.

That is what I'd say
to the Little Black boy
who I call ...   my son.

Discussion Questions

1. What do you know about race in America?

2. How does the author describe the little boy in the poem? Why do you think the author describes him this way?

3. What is the author asking the little boy to do? Why is the little boy being asked to do these things? Is this fair to the little boy?

4. What can the little boy do in the poem? What can't the little boy do in the poem? How do these two things compare?

5. Who do you think is writing to the little boy? If you were the little boy in this poem, who would be writing this to you? Would you listen to this person and the advice they are sharing?
Why or why not?

6. Do you think the little boy in this poem could also be a little girl? Why or why not?

7. If you were the author, and you wanted to help someone you love stay safe in America, what would you tell them to do? Why?

LittleBlackBoy.org

Dr.

About the Author

Cheri Langley, MPH, CHES, is a wife to her husband of 11 years and a mother of two young Black children, including her six-year-old daughter and four-year-old son. She is a self-proclaimed writer and advocate for social and political justice. Her life work has been working with socially disadvantaged populations; particularly Black adolescents and their families.

For the past 20 years, Dr. Langley has been involved in practice and research involving HIV/AIDS, and STI awareness and prevention and adolescent youth risk behavior. Dr. Langley also has a great deal of experience in community based participatory approaches, particularly in underserved and minority populations.

She is a lover of Jesus Christ who believes that all men have been created equal, regardless of their past or present circumstances, and should be treated as such, particularly, regardless of their race or ethnicity. It is her life work to create social change in the environment around her through her work in the behavioral sciences, as well as her work through the written word. As a native of Louisville, KY, she currently resides in her hometown with her husband and children.

Cheri Langley

The Illustrators

Randy Gray II

Randy Gray II is a cartoonist and caricature artist from Louisville, KY. He is a graduate of duPont Manual HighSchool's Visual Art program, and earned a BA in Graphic Arts from the University of Kentucky. Since graduating, Randy has administered several online comic strips including randygraycomics, My Quest for Cool (an auto-biographical strip), and Lil Dude, which was transformed into a self-published comic series entitled, 'Lil Dude and Rooney' an exploration of Black History that has been added to Jefferson County Public School Libraries. Randy has conducted workshops on cartooning and comic book creation for summer camps and held a month long artist residency at the Louisville Free Public Library. Most recently, he has been illustrating children's books and working as a caricaturist for local events and parties. Randy has a wife and three children, loves to exercise, draw, and spend time his family.

Christa Harris is a professional visual artist residing in Louisville, KY who sold her first print at the age of 12. This linoleum block print rendering of the iconic civil rights activist, Malcolm. X shaped her voice as an artist and catapulted the importance of Black representation in her work.

In 2002, she earned a BFA with emphasis in Painting & Graphic Design from the University of Kentucky. Then, in 2017, she illustrated and copublished the children's book *My Magical Hair*, available on Amazon in collaboration with the book's author, Nina Reid. She has curated and exhibited in various shows and festivals in her hometown, including *RAW, Natural Born Artists Showcase.*

Christa is currently working towards her Masters in Arts Administration at the University of Kentucky, and is in pursuit of a second Masters in Art Therapy which she anticpates to obtain from the University of Louisville. She also works as a Market Specialist intern for the nonprofit orgnization, Art Inc. Kentucky, in an effort to establish its Louisville base. She aspires to earn a PhD in Arts Administration from the University of Kentucky, and eventually own and operate a gallery with private practice nestled within.

Joe Goodwin Photography

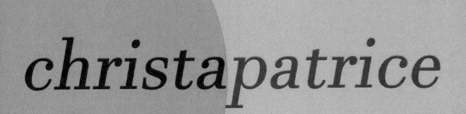

christapatrice

Made in the USA
Columbia, SC
14 September 2021

45468602R00022